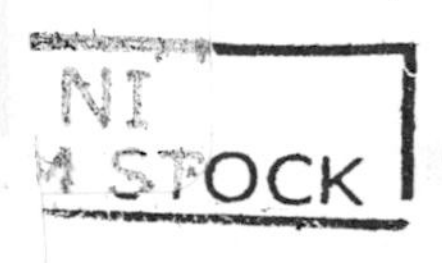

For Alex (who saved the day!)
and Sam ~ M.S.

For all the wonderful and
misunderstood sharks in the sea ~ S.C.

BLOOMSBURY CHILDREN'S BOOKS
Bloomsbury Publishing Plc
50 Bedford Square, London, WC1B 3DP, UK
BLOOMSBURY, BLOOMSBURY CHILDREN'S BOOKS and the Diana logo are trademarks of Bloomsbury Publishing Plc
First published in Great Britain by Bloomsbury Publishing Plc

A catalogue record for this book is available from the British Library

ISBN 978 1 4088 9782 9 (HB)
ISBN 978 1 4088 9781 2 (PB)
ISBN 978 1 4088 9783 6 (eBook)

1 3 5 7 9 10 8 6 4 2

Printed and bound in China by Leo Paper Products, Heshan, Guandong
All papers used by Bloomsbury Publishing Plc are natural, recyclable products from wood grown in well managed forests.
The manufacturing processes conform to the environmental regulations of the country of origin.

To find out more about our authors and books visit www.bloomsbury.com and sign up for our newsletters

SANTA
JAWS
Mark SPERRING
Sophie CORRIGAN
BLOOMSBURY
CHILDREN'S BOOKS
LONDON OXFORD NEW YORK NEW DELHI SYDNEY

Down beneath the ocean waves,
it's almost Christmas Eve,
and a sneaky shark named **Shelly**
has something **FESTIVE** up her sleeve.

She's bought herself a Santa hat
from the Deep Sea Christmas Store...

Then made herself a JOLLY sign
to hang on her front door.
Welcome to
Santa's Grotto!
Little fishes PLEASE come in,
and meet the real life
SANTA CLAUS.
It's really, REALLY him!

Now, MOST fish know
where Shelly lives,
and think she's
FULL OF TRICKS.
And, after looking at that sign,

they swim off

EXTRA quick!

But one day, through some tangled weeds,
a squid named Sid passed by.

And when he read that jolly sign
he gave a happy cry...

"Well! I've never hung a Christmas star

or licked a candy cane,

and I've never built a snowman,

(which seems an awful shame).

But today's my LUCKY, LUCKY day.

Golly, whizz and gee!

For GUESS WHO's meeting Santa Claus . . ."

"Yes, me!
Yes, me!

YES, ME!"

So that excited squid
named Sid gave the
driftwood door a

KNOCK.

And when it swished
right open...

it gave
him quite
a shock.

"Come in . . ."
called a KINDLY voice,
"I'm here, right at the back.
So swim a
little closer . . .
I've got presents
in my sack!"

"Presents!" squealed little Sid.

"I'm happy as a clam!

Who's going to meet
SANTA CLAUS?

I AM!

I AM!

I AM!"

But, there in the darkness,
was all quite as it seemed?

When little Sid swam closer,
he gave a squid-like scream.

"Why's your skin all GREY and SHINY,
and where are your fur-trimmed boots?"
Said Shelly with a
Ho-ho-ho!
"I'm in my
diving suit!"
"But your teeth are SHARP
and POINTY,"
Sid spluttered in the dark.
"You're NOT the
REAL Santa Claus–
you're a great, big, sharp-toothed . . .

. . . shark!"

Sid **kicked** and **flicked** his tentacles,

too scared to stick around.

But, as he swam to safety, there came a

sobbing

sound.

"I didn't want to eat you,"

called Shelly
through
her tears.

"All I really
wanted was
to spread
SOME
YULETIDE
CHEER!"

"So, please, PLEASE
won't you trust me?
I'm TRULY not all bad.
Will you help me
give the ocean
the best Christmas
that it's had?"

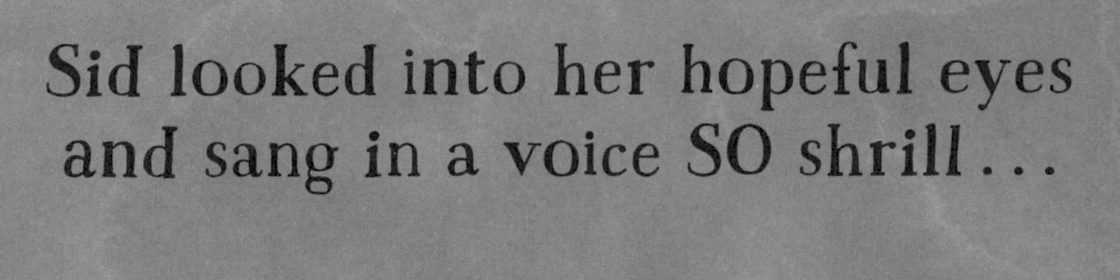

Sid looked into her hopeful eyes
and sang in a voice SO shrill . . .

"Will I TRUST YOU?
Will I HELP YOU?

HMMMM . . ."

“I WILL!

I WILL!

I WILL!"

Then, all across the ocean

presents slowly drifted down.

Through icy depths

and seaweed groves,

right here to

CORAL TOWN!

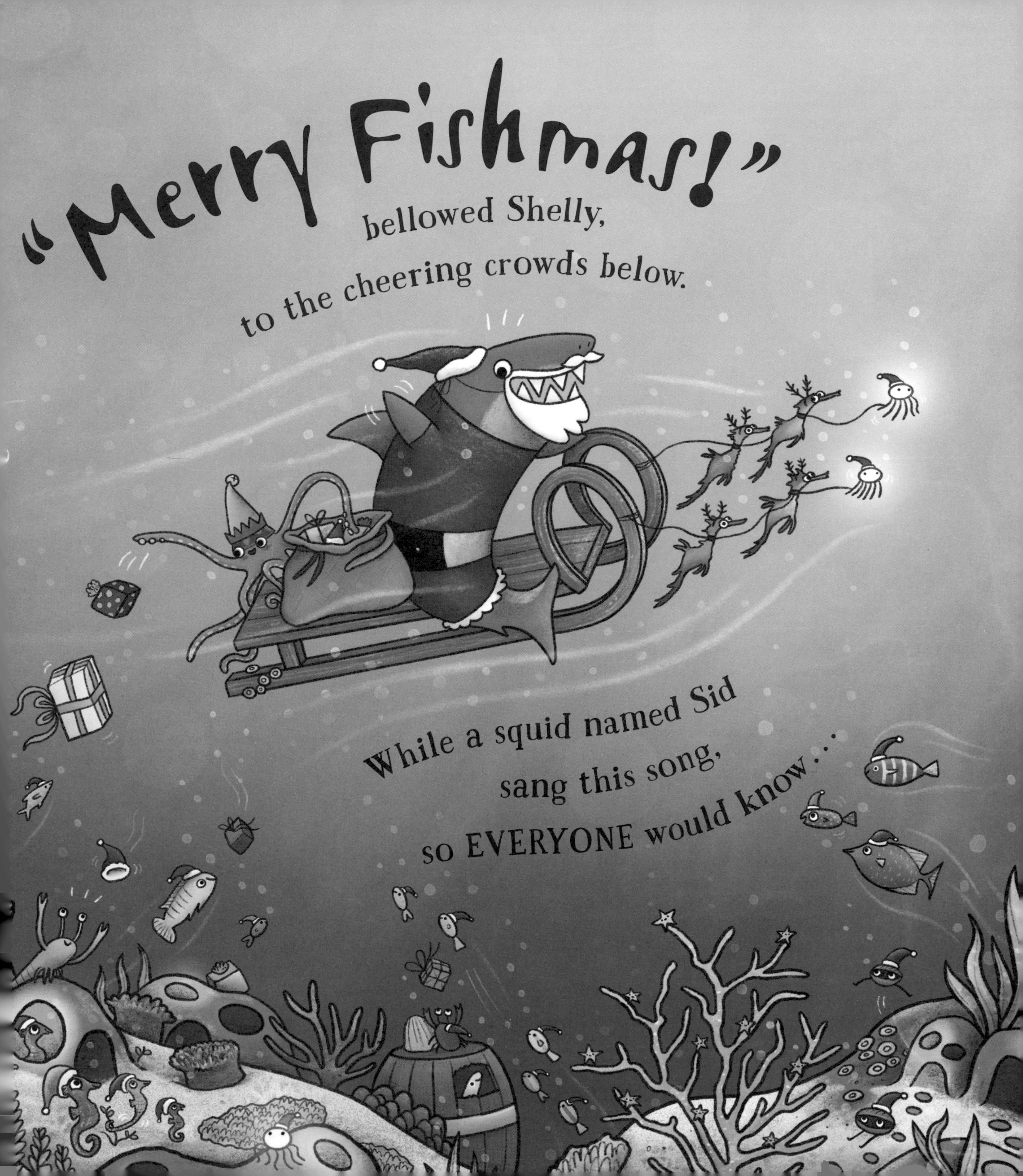

"Merry Fishmas!"

bellowed Shelly,

to the cheering crowds below.

While a squid named Sid

sang this song,

so EVERYONE would know . . .

"I've never hung a Christmas star

or licked a candy cane,

and I've never built a snowman,

(which seems like quite a shame).

And though I've not met Santa Claus,
I'm STILL a LUCKY squid . . .
For, who just met
SANTA JAWS?"

"I DID!
I DID!

I DID!"